THE LOST LAKE

ALLEN SAY

Scholastic Inc.
New York   Toronto   London   Auckland   Sydney

For Cort Conley

ISBN 0-590-46784-0

Copyright © 1989 by Allen Say.
All rights reserved. Published by Scholastic Inc., 730 Broadway, New York, NY 10003, by arrangement with Houghton Mifflin Company.

12 11 10 9 8 7 6 5 4 3 2 1   3 4 5 6 7 8/9

Printed in the U.S.A.   08

First Scholastic printing, January 1993

THE LOST LAKE

I went to live with Dad last summer.

Every day he worked in his room from morning to night, sometimes on weekends, too. Dad wasn't much of a talker, but when he was busy he didn't talk at all.

I didn't know anybody in the city, so I stayed home most of the time. It was too hot to play outside anyway. In one month I finished all the books I'd brought and grew tired of watching TV.

One morning I started cutting pictures out of old magazines, just to be doing something. They were pictures of mountains and rivers and lakes, and some showed people fishing and canoeing. Looking at them made me feel cool, so I pinned them up in my room.

Dad didn't notice them for two days. When he did, he looked at them one by one.

"Nice pictures," he said.

"Are you angry with me, Dad?" I asked, because he saved old magazines for his work.

"It's all right, Luke," he said. "I'm having this place painted soon anyway."

He thought I was talking about the marks I'd made on the wall.

That Saturday Dad woke me up early in the morning and told me we were going camping! I was wide awake in a second. He gave me a pair of brand-new hiking boots to try out. They were perfect.

In the hallway I saw a big backpack and a knapsack all packed and ready to go.

"What's in them, Dad?" I asked.

"Later," he said. "We have a long drive ahead of us."

In the car I didn't ask any more questions because Dad was so grumpy in the morning.

"Want a sip?" he said, handing me his mug. He'd never let me drink coffee before. It had lots of sugar in it.

"Where are we going?" I finally asked.

"We're off to the Lost Lake, my lad."

"How can you lose a lake?"

"No one's found it, that's how." Dad was smiling! "Grandpa and I used to go there a long time ago. It was our special place, so don't tell any of your friends."

"I'll never tell," I promised. "How long are we going to stay there?"

"Five days, maybe a week."

"We're going to sleep outside for a whole week?"

"That's the idea."

"Oh, boy!"

We got to the mountains in the afternoon.

"It's a bit of a hike to the lake, son," Dad said.

"I don't mind," I told him. "Are there any fish in the lake?"

"Hope so. We'll have to catch our dinner, you know."

"You didn't bring any food?"

"Of course not. We're going to live like true outdoorsmen."

"Oh . . ."

Dad saw my face and started to laugh. He must have been joking. I didn't think we were going very far anyway, because Dad's pack was so heavy I couldn't even lift it.

Well, Dad was like a mountain goat. He went straight up
the trail, whistling all the while. But I was gasping in no time.
My knapsack got very heavy and I started to fall behind.

Dad stopped for me often, but he wouldn't let me
take off my pack. If I did I'd be too tired to go on, he said.
It was almost suppertime when we got to the lake.

The place reminded me of the park near Dad's apartment. He wasn't whistling or humming anymore.

"Welcome to the *Found* Lake," he muttered from the side of his mouth.

"What's wrong, Dad?"

"Do you want to camp with all these people around us?"

"I don't mind."

"Well, I do!"

"Are we going home?"

"Of course not!"

He didn't even take off his pack. He just turned and started to walk away.

Soon the lake was far out of sight.

Then it started to rain. Dad gave me a poncho and it kept
me dry, but I wondered where we were going to sleep that night.
I wondered what we were going to do for dinner. I wasn't sure
about camping anymore.

I was glad when Dad finally stopped and set up the tent.
The rain and wind beat against it, but we were warm and cozy
inside. And Dad had brought food. For dinner we had salami
and dried apricots.

"I'm sorry about the lake, Dad," I said.

He shook his head. "You know something, Luke? There aren't any secret places left in the world anymore."

"What if we go very far up in the mountains? Maybe we can find our own lake."

"There are lots of lakes up here, but that one was special."

"But we've got a whole week, Dad."

"Well, why not? Maybe we'll find a lake that's not on the map."

"Sure, we will!"

We started early in the morning. When the fog cleared we
saw other hikers ahead of us. Sure enough, Dad became very glum.

"We're going cross-country, partner," he said.

"Won't we get lost?"

"A wise man never leaves home without his compass."

So we went off the trail. The hills went on and on. The
mountains went on and on. It was kind of lonesome. It seemed
as if Dad and I were the only people left in the world.
And then we hiked into a big forest.

At noontime we stopped by a creek and ate lunch and drank ice-cold water straight from the stream. I threw rocks in the water, and fish, like shadows, darted in the pools.

"Isn't this a good place to camp, Dad?"

"I thought we were looking for our lake."

"Yes, right . . ." I mumbled.

The forest went on and on.

"I don't mean to scare you, son," Dad said. "But we're in bear country. We don't want to surprise them, so we have to make a lot of noise. If they hear us, they'll just go away."

What a time to tell me! I started to shout as loudly as I could. Even Dad wouldn't be able to beat off bears. I thought about those people having fun back at the lake. I thought about the creek, too, with all those fish in it. That would have been a fine place to camp. The Lost Lake hadn't been so bad either.

It was dark when we got out of the forest. We built a fire
and that made me feel better. Wild animals wouldn't come near
a fire. Dad cooked beef stroganoff and it was delicious.

Later it was bedtime. The sleeping bag felt wonderful. Dad
and I started to count the shooting stars, then I worried that maybe
we weren't going to find our lake.

"What are you thinking about, Luke?" Dad asked.

"I didn't know you could cook like that," I said.

Dad laughed. "That was only freeze-dried stuff. When we get
home, I'll cook you something really special."

"You know something, Dad? You seem like a different person
up here."

"Better or worse?"

"A lot better."

"How so?"

"You talk more."

"I'll have to talk more often, then."

That made me smile. Then I slept.

Dad shook me awake. The sun was just coming up, turning everything all gold and orange and yellow. And there was the lake, right in front of us.

For a long time we watched the light change on the water, getting brighter and brighter. Dad didn't say a word the whole time. But then, I didn't have anything to say either.

After breakfast we climbed a mountain and saw our lake below us. There wasn't a sign of people anywhere. It really seemed as if Dad and I were all alone in the world.

I liked it just fine.